The Genie

by

Mary Hooper

Illustrated by Kirstin Holbrow

First published in Great Britain by Barrington Stoke Ltd
10 Belford Terrace, Edinburgh, EH4 3DQ
Copyright © 1999 Mary Hooper
Illustrations © Kirstin Holbrow
The moral right of the author has been asserted in
accordance with the Copyright, Designs and
Patents Act 1988
ISBN 1-902260-20-1
Printed by Polestar AUP Aberdeen Ltd

MEET THE AUTHOR - MARY HOOPER

What is your favourite animal?
A cat
What is your favourite boy's name?
Rowan
What is your favourite girl's name?
Bethany (this week!)
What is your favourite food?
Seafood
What is your favourite music?
Rolling Stones
What is your favourite hobby?
Pottering about

MEET THE ILLUSTRATOR - KIRSTIN HOLBROW

What is your favourite animal?
My dog, Pewter Plum
What is your favourite boy's name?
George
What is your favourite girl's name?
Beryl
What is your favourite food?
Shellfish
What is your favourite music?
Ambient Techno
What is your favourite hobby?
Rowing on the River Wye

Barrington Stoke was a famous and much-loved story-teller. He travelled from village to village carrying a lantern to light his way. He arrived as it grew dark and when the young boys and girls of the village saw the glow of his lantern, they hurried to the central meeting place. They were full of excitement and expectation, for his stories were always wonderful.

Then Barrington Stoke set down his lantern. In the flickering light the listeners were enthralled by his tales of adventure, horror and mystery. He knew exactly what they liked best and he loved telling a good story. And another. And then another. When the lantern burned low and dawn was nearly breaking, he slipped away. He was gone by morning, only to appear the next day in some other village to tell the next story.

Contents

Chapter 1
Dad's Birthday Present

My sister Sarah and I were at a jumble sale in the village hall. It was our Dad's birthday soon. As we were both broke, we'd gone there to try and find a present for him.

"Hey, Fudge, have you found anything yet?" Sarah asked me, looking over my shoulder onto the white elephant stall. The table was covered in useless junk.

1

I stared at the chipped mugs, the plastic plates and the tin trays with half their pictures worn away.

"Nothing," I said. "Not a thing."

"Ah ha!" Sarah said suddenly. "I've just seen something ..."

She leapt away from me and started to burrow in a pile of old furniture on the next stall along.

I stared at the jumble in front of me and then I noticed a small box. It was painted dark blue, and had a silvery moon on the top and stars all over. Would Dad like it? I picked it up and frowned at it.

Maybe ...

"Do you want that, dear?" said the woman behind the counter. "You can have it for twenty pence."

That decided it.

"Sold!" I said.

Well, Dad didn't expect much from us. Just as well, really. I paid and backed away from the stall. I looked at the box more closely. When I lifted the lid, I found a tiny scroll of paper inside. I smoothed it out, and read, in faded writing,

> To call out the spirit of the box –
> tap G-E-N-I-E in Morse code. To send him back, tap GENIE backwards E-I-N-E-G.

I frowned. What did *that* mean? Some sort of joke, of course.

I closed the lid and ran my fingers over the stars. It was really quite pretty, though ...

"What's that tatty old thing?" Sarah was next to me again.

"What's it look like?" I snapped.

From this sisterly exchange you will see at once that Sarah and I don't exactly get on. You'd be right. She's a year older than me, and a year bossier. She tries to push me around.

"It looks like a dirty old box," Sarah said. Her voice rose in disgust. "You haven't bought that for Dad, have you?"

"I might have done," I replied.

"Well, how mean can you get?" Sarah smiled smugly. "Guess what I've bought him? The *best* present! Something fantastic!" She held up a big clumsy thing with dangling lead and a plug. "A trouser press! He's always wanted one."

I rolled my eyes.

"Big deal," I said.

"You haven't really bought him that old box thing, have you?" she said. She added, "He won't like that but he's going to *love* what I've got."

"Well, hooray - hoo - blooming - ray for you," I said.

Chapter 2
A Sight for Sore Eyes?

Two days later I was in my bedroom sitting at my desk. I was supposed to be doing homework but I just happened to have *The Wonderful World of Knowledge* on my bed. And it just happened to be open at the page headed Morse code.

I wasn't going to do anything. I mean, I didn't believe for a moment what that little scroll of paper in the box had said.

I was getting on with my homework. Sarah and I were in the same history group in our village school and had the same topic work to do – Write three pages on 'Schools in Victorian England'. Of course she'd done hers. Sometimes, though, I glanced at the blue box on my desk and thought *what if ...*

I told myself not to be silly.

But just suppose ...

My hand reached out for the box. I quickly withdrew it again.

But it wouldn't hurt just to try ...

Quickly, before I could talk myself out of it, I picked up the box. I pulled *The Wonderful World of Knowledge* towards me and copied out the letters G-E-N-I and E in Morse code. Then I tapped out G-E-N-I-E on the lid of the box.

When I had finished, I felt a bit silly. I was just about to go back to the Victorians, when there was a tiny sparky noise and a puff of smoke. I noticed an odd smell like cheap perfume.

And then a voice said, "Oh dearie me. Some mistake. This certainly isn't a scented palace in Arabia."

I jumped, turned and there he was, a chubby little man circled with mist, wearing a brilliant blue cloak and puffy trousers in some shiny material. He had long, twirly shoes with bells on them, and was loaded down with gold jewellery. He was a bit of a show-off, actually, a cross between a wizard and a circus clown.

"Who are you?" we both said together.

He bowed low. "I am the Genie of the Box."

"D-don't be silly," I said. "You can't be!"

"I am," he said. "And who are you ...?"

"Fiona," I stuttered. "Usually called Fudge."

"Princess Fudge?" he asked.

"No. Just Miss."

He raised his eyebrows. "I usually work for princesses, sultans and rajahs."

And then he looked round at the mess of my bedroom – at the scruffy wallpaper, the apple cores lying on the floor and the dirty mugs on my desk. He raised his eyebrows even higher.

"I usually work in splendid palaces, castles and ivory towers," he said.

"S-sorry," I said, still hardly believing it. "This time you've got me and 12 Arnott Avenue. It's a three-bedroomed semi," I added helpfully, "and I live here with my sister Sarah and my Dad."

"And have you got two hundred servants?" he asked.

I shook my head.

"No room," I said.

All the time I was speaking I was thinking that this just wasn't possible. The whole thing was mad and I must be dreaming.

While I was thinking *that*, though, another bit of me was thinking that if he was a genie, then wow, wouldn't it be fantastic! A genie could get me things, jewels and gold and a red sports car and *anything*. He could take me for a ride on a magic carpet, grant me three wishes ...

"Are you actually, really, properly a genie?" I asked.

He bowed deeply and the mist around him shimmered. "I am, oh Highness, oh Magnificent One! And may your camels never go lame, may your jewelled palaces increase in ..." He stopped and looked around. "That's a bit over the top for round here, isn't it? I mean, we aren't exactly talking jewelled palaces. And I don't suppose you've even seen a real live camel."

"I certainly have," I said. "At London Zoo, two years ago."

Three wishes, I was thinking. A decent present for Dad, a fantastic designer outfit or two, and a mountain bike. Sorted.

"Er ... is it true that genies can grant three wishes?" I asked nicely. I mean, I didn't want to sound greedy or anything.

"Of course, oh Mistress of the Moonbeams," said Genie, bowing low.

"Brilliant!" I said. Three wishes! What a result. "Can I have them now, please?"

"Just as you desire, oh Princess of the Ponies."

"Thanks a lot," I said. Having a genie around was going to be pretty okay ...

Chapter 3
Wish upon a Star ...

I was just about to give him my three wishes when Genie clapped his hands. There was a big puff of smoke and suddenly – *suddenly* – there were three old women in tall, black hats in my room. Three weird old bats with warts on their chins wearing dark, raggedy cloaks and holding broomsticks. I gave a shriek.

"Here are your three witches, oh Daughter of the Dalmatians!" announced Genie.

The three witches gave horrid cackles.

"By eye of toad and cat's rear botty ..." one began.

"Not *witches*," I cried. "Wishes. I distinctly said three wishes!"

Genie rolled his eyes. "Oh, dearie me," he said. "Do you wish these witches gone?"

"Yes, please!"

"All three of them? You don't want to keep one for the occasional spell and sorcery?"

"Definitely not."

"That'll be two wishes used up, you know ..."

"Never mind that!" I said in panic, because one witch was rubbing her hands together and looking as if she'd like to put me into a cauldron.

Genie looked a bit put out, but he clapped his hands. All three of them disappeared as suddenly as they'd come, leaving behind a whiff of old bonfires.

I sat down on my bed, feeling faint.

"Do you want your last wish now, oh Protector of the Polecats?" Genie asked.

I breathed deeply. "Just give me a second ..."

Just then, *just* as I was thinking about whether to have a mountain bike or a present for Dad, my bedroom door was flung open.

There stood Sarah.

She looked at me, looked at him, and screamed. "Wha ...wha ... what's that little fat whatsit doing here?"

"He's just a friend!" I said quickly.

"That's not a friend! That's one of those things from Aladdin! That's a ... a genie!" And she screamed again.

"Can't you do something?!" I said to Genie urgently. "This is my sister and she's going to make a terrible fuss. My Dad will come running up and more than likely you'll be taken off and investigated. You'll never get back in that box again."

Straight away, Genie raised his arm and pointed his little finger at Sarah. There was a sparkly flash from his fingertip and suddenly Sarah went quiet. She was still standing in the doorway and her mouth was open as if she was screaming, but she was silent and still.

"Wh ... what's happened?" I asked. "She looks as if she's been frozen."

"Almost, oh Ruler of the Reindeer," said Genie. "I've freeze-framed her."

He gave a little bow. "It's the latest thing. All the rage with genies nowadays."

"You don't say ..." I said faintly.

Chapter 4
A Close Shave

I went over and waved my hand in Sarah's face. She didn't even blink. I poked out my tongue at her, called her a toad, and she didn't even quiver.

"Do you want her to stay like it?" Genie asked. "It would be a fitting end for someone who called a genie a little fat whatsit."

For a moment I thought about how lovely that would be. I thought about not having her on my back all the time, and how the teachers at school wouldn't be able to say, 'Such a pity you're not more like your sister' and stuff like that.

But then I thought about all the explaining I'd have to do. Having a sister freeze-framed in your bedroom doorway wouldn't make for an easy life.

"No," I sighed with regret. "You'd better start her up again."

"So do you want a rewind, oh Monarch of the Mules? Back to the moment she opened the door?"

I nodded. "That would be good."

"We have all the modern knowledges," said Genie. "We are most hip and happening."

"But you'll have to go back in the box first, won't you?"

He bowed and nodded. "Before I do so," he said, "are there any other tasks you wish me to perform?"

"I'm not sure," I said slowly. I didn't want to use up my last wish without really thinking about it. "Er ... are tasks different from wishes?"

Genie nodded. "Tasks are more your everyday jobs," he said. "Moving palaces across mountain ranges, turning seas into liquid gold – that's your typical task."

"Oh. I see," I said. But I didn't really see the difference.

The other thing was that fabulous happenings might be okay in Arabian Nights, but would be difficult to hide in 12 Arnott Avenue. I mean, it was going to be hard enough to explain where a new mountain bike had come from, let alone tell Dad that we were going to live in a 300-room castle.

"Perhaps just a *small* task to start with," I said. My glance fell on my school books. "Like, could you do me three pages of topic work on 'Schools in Victorian England'?"

Genie pointed his little finger. There was a tiny flash and a curl of smoke appeared over my topic work book. "Done!"

"Brilliant." I glanced at Sarah, set solid as a statue in the doorway. "And now her ..."

Genie pointed. "I'll do her on a delayed action setting, oh Mistress of the Monkeys," he said. "And then you have two minutes to get me back in the box."

I pulled over *The Wonderful World of Knowledge*. "Thank you very much. I'll be calling on you again soon," I said. Just as soon as I'd worked out what to ask for.

I tapped out GENIE backwards, E-I-N-E-G, in Morse code. Genie went into a spiral of smoke and got smaller and smaller until he disappeared into the box. He left behind him just a wisp of smoke and a spark.

A few seconds later, Sarah started moving.

"What's that?!" she said.

"What's what?" I looked up with an innocent grin from *The Wonderful World of Knowledge.*

She screwed up her face, bewildered, looking all round.

"Er ... just what's ... er ... *something* ..." She was talking nonsense. "I can't think what I was going to say. I'm sure it was important though."

"It's all that homework you do," I said. "It's probably scrambled your brain."

Her glance fell on *The Wonderful World of Knowledge*. "Why are you reading *that*? I've never seen you even look at it before."

"There's a lot you don't know about me," I said. "I'm a very private person."

She looked around the room again.

"There's something funny going on ... I thought I heard a noise in here and when I came in ..." She screwed up her face. "It's like a dream or something. I thought I saw a little ... I can't quite remember."

"I should go and have a nice lie down," I said soothingly.

"I was going to ask you about Dad's birthday. You're not really giving him that old box, are you?"

I glanced at the blue box. The very special blue box. "No," I said. "I thought I'd get him a tape for the car."

"Well, as an extra present I thought we could do some jobs. Divide the household chores between us and do them for a week."

"Okay, okay," I said, just wanting her to go. "You sort it out and write me a list."

With Genie around, household chores would be a piece of cake.

Chapter 5
A Little Language Trouble

Sarah, looking fresh as a daisy, walked beside me on our way to school. I looked at her, then tugged at my jumper so that it went baggy at the bottom and slouched a little as I walked. There's something about Sarah which makes me want to do this.

"Now, here's the list of jobs," she said. "I've ticked all the ones I'm going to do."

I glanced at the list. She'd ticked all the decent ones, of course, like shopping and vacuuming. I'd got the horrible ones like changing the sheets and ironing Dad's shirts.

I stuffed the list into my school bag.

"Have you done your topic work, then?" Sarah asked.

I patted my school bag. I hadn't even looked at it. I had forgotten all about it, actually. "Course I have!"

"Mine's really good," she said. "I'll probably get an A+ for it."

"Big deal," I said.

We had to give in our homework first thing that morning, so I didn't think any more about mine until the afternoon. Our teacher, Hoppy Hopkins, was at the front, marking homework, when she suddenly bellowed my name. "Fiona Busby!" she roared. Just like that.

I stood up.

"What's this?" she asked, waving my homework book.

"Er ... three pages on Victorian schools?" I said nervously.

"It might well be," Hoppy said. "But why is it written in a foreign language?"

"Is it?" I squeaked.

"Don't get clever with me, young lady. You've handed in three pages written in Arabic."

"Ah," I said. *Yeochh*! I screamed inside. Genie had done my homework all right, but he'd done it in his own language!

I thought quickly. "Er ..., what happened was, I hurt my hand at the weekend and dictated my homework to my cousin to write."

"And he's an Arab, is he?"

I nodded, not looking at Sarah. Not even she would rat on me to a teacher though.

"Is he an *ancient* Arab?" Hoppy asked, deadly calm.

"What?"

"This homework is written in a form of Arabic which was last used five hundred years ago."

I sighed heavily.

"I suppose you thought you'd have a bit of fun with me, did you?"

I looked at Hoppy. The chances of having fun with her would be as likely as buying a wooden box for twenty pence and finding a genie inside. What did I just say? ... Well, let's just say it was pretty unlikely.

"Did you copy it from some tomb in a museum?" Hoppy asked.

I thought it best to go along with this. "That's right," I said. "A tomb. I thought it would be interesting for you. I know you like old languages."

"I like homework I can read," she said. "Stay in after school every night until you've done it."

*****

Of course, I had Sarah onto me for the rest of the day then, asking to see the homework and pestering me all the time. In the end I had to flush it down the loo and refuse to talk any more about it.

When I got home (late, of course) I raced upstairs, got Genie out and told him what had happened.

"Apologies, oh Daughter of the Dawn," he said, bowing and swirling around me. "May I be scraped with a thousand razors, may my camels collapse!"

"Never mind all that," I said. "Can you just do some household tasks when I'm at school tomorrow?"

"Of course, oh Keeper of the Kangaroos!"

I heard Sarah coming up the stairs and looked at the list of jobs she'd given me.

"I've got to rush now," I said quickly, "but I want you to dust the furniture and change the beds. Is that clear?"

"Perfectly, oh Mistress of the Mongooses!"

"Oh, and make Dad a nice birthday cake too, please."

I tapped him back in – not a moment too soon, because Sarah opened my door and peered in.

"I thought I heard you speaking to someone."

"I wandered lonely as a frog, that sits upon a wooden log," I said, and then looked up with pretend surprise. "Oh, I didn't see you there. I was reciting some of my poetry."

"I thought I heard two voices!" Sarah sniffed the air. "And there's a funny smoky smell."

"I was ... er ... just practising lighting camp fires, for when I join the Guides," I said.

"What?!" exclaimed Sarah.

"Only joking!" I said hastily.

"Hmm," she said. "Something very funny is going on around here ..."

Chapter 6
All Change

I was late in again the next afternoon because of staying to finish the topic work. Sarah, luckily, had gone to a friend's house so I was home first. And that was just as well.

I went into the sitting room, looked round and gave a yelp of surprise. The furniture had been dusted all right, *dusted with gold dust!* A thick layer of shimmering powder lay over every bit of furniture. The sofa and chairs, mantelpiece and window frames gleamed softly. Even the goldfish bowl glowed with gold.

I squashed down a scream, shut the sitting room door firmly behind me and ran upstairs into my bedroom.

Or tried to. I couldn't run very far, though, because there was a bed in the way. Not my bed but a huge, new bed with thick, wooden posts at each corner and a frilly roof. It had great big, flowery curtains, and a sickly green and gold jewelled bedspread over it.

I backed away, horrified, and went to
Sarah's room. *Her* bed was now a vast
hammock, covered with thick, fur rugs, held in
the air by four stuffed bears.

Dad's bed was a big, blue mattress high in the air, supported by four tall, marble columns twined round with plaster angels.

Change the beds, I'd said. *Dust the furniture*.

And that's just what Genie had done.

I ran back to my room, clambered over the bed and reached the box to tap him out.

"Yes, oh Highness of the Hyenas!" he said, appearing on top of a jewelled pillow.

"Those household tasks!" I panted, out of breath.

"My work is magnificent, is it not, oh Mover of Mountains?" he said. "Is the sitting room not covered in best quality gold dust? Are the beds not full of glory?"

"Oh, they're glorious all right," I said, "but I'm afraid you've got things slightly wrong."

And I explained about dusting and changing, and said that I wanted the original ones back as soon as possible.

Genie looked put out. "As you wish, oh Daughter of the Donkeys," he sniffed, and suddenly I was lying on my old bed.

"Are *all* the beds back?" I asked. "And the gold dust gone?"

He nodded, tight-lipped.

I breathed a sigh of relief and had just tapped him back in when there was a scream from downstairs.

"Fiona!" Sarah shrilled. "This cake! Where ever did you get it? What does it mean?"

The cake! I hadn't even looked at it.

"I made it!" I said, galloping down. "Bet you wish you'd thought of it!"

I stopped dead as I went into the kitchen. The cake was about the size of a double wardrobe.

It was the sort of cake you'd have if you were expecting three thousand people to tea. It was iced in blue and green and covered with silver balls and coloured sweets. Across the top, in bright pink icing, it said, BIRTHDAY GRITTINGS TO FATHER OF FUDGE, KEEPER OF THE GENIE.

"I don't understand! What's happening and ..." said Sarah.

"Ah," I said, "just a sec."

And *then* I had to dash upstairs, get Genie out again, get him to freeze-frame Sarah, ask him to change the cake and replace it for a small jam sponge, and so on.

I tell you, I was worn out. Life was getting *very* complicated.

Chapter 7
A Gigantic Problem

"You see, we don't often wear belly dancing outfits over here," I explained to Genie a few days later. "Certainly we don't wear them to parties."

I'd given Genie the task of finding me an outfit because I was stuck for something to wear for a meal out on Dad's birthday. When it had turned up it had fringes, beads, dangling jewels and not a lot else.

"But it was a most hip and happening outfit!" Genie protested. "My other princesses have ..."

"Yes, well, what your other princesses might wear isn't right for round here," I said. "And now if you'll excuse me, I have to go downstairs and change the goldfish."

Genie's eyes gleamed. "Change it for a shark?"

"Change its water!" I said. "You have to do that once a week. It's not much of a pet," I muttered, "but it's all Dad will let me have. Wish I could have something decent." I thought longingly of a horse, or a boxer dog, or a big, fluffy cat. Maybe, when I'd got Genie trained up a bit ...

Sarah was in the kitchen. She yelled at me that I had to go and help with the washing up *now*. So I tapped Genie back into the box and went down.

I was the one left with the drying, of course. And then Sarah said I had to peel the potatoes. We were just getting into a row about it when I heard a noise from upstairs. A strange noise. Well, it's not everyday that you hear an elephant trumpeting from your bedroom, is it?

"What was *that*?" Sarah asked, shocked.

"Er ... was it thunder?"

"Course it wasn't thunder. It sounded like an animal. It sounded like ..."

The trumpeting came again.

"I'll go up!" I said. "Perhaps ... er ... one of my books has fallen off the shelf."

I dashed up the stairs two at a time and burst into my bedroom. At least, I tried to burst

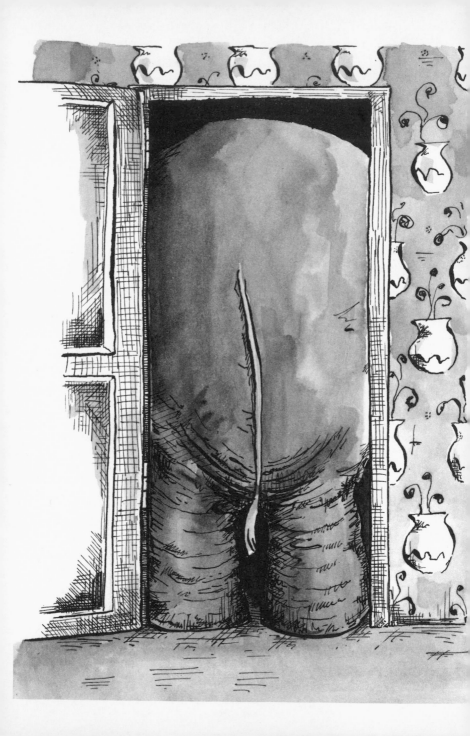

into my bedroom, but there was an elephant's bottom in the way.

I screamed.

"What *is* it?" Sarah called fearfully from downstairs.

I tried to recover myself.

"Oh ... er ... next door's cat's in here," I said. "He's been jumping about and er ... making a noise. I'll catch him. Here, pussy, pussy!"

I squeezed through a gap in the door, then dropped on all fours to get through the elephant's legs and reach Genie's box.

"What's happened?" I squealed when he appeared. "What's this elephant doing in my room?"

"Not a lot at the moment," Genie said. "It's a bit restricted for space."

"But why is it here?" I gasped. "I never asked for an elephant."

"You wished for a decent pet, oh Daughter of the Dolphins," said Genie mildly. "It was such a large wish that it took a while to fulfil."

"But I didn't realise I'd wished for anything! I mean, it's not really suitable ... Whatever kind of a person has an elephant for a pet?"

"A *princess* kind of person," Genie said in a meaningful tone of voice.

"Oh," I said.

The elephant moved its rear end and pushed me across the room.

"Look," I said hurriedly, "I'm sorry about this, but I'm really not a princess kind of person at all. Most of all where pets are concerned."

"Do you wish me to return it?" Genie asked stiffly.

"Yes, please," I said. I patted a bit of elephant. "It's very nice, of course, but not really suitable for a small bedroom."

"I see," said Genie.

"Fiona!" Sarah's voice came from outside my door. "Why can't I get in? What's happening?"

"Nothing! Everything's okay. Just putting the cat back out of the window – *Here, puss.*" I dropped my voice to a whisper. "If you could get rid of it now, please."

Still looking very cross, Genie raised both hands towards the elephant. There was a fizzing noise and a flash of fire and it disappeared.

I began to tap Genie back in.

"Sorry," I said to him. "I mean, it was a nice thought and everything, but I just haven't got the space."

Genie bowed. "Such a large wish," he said. "Any leftovers will disappear over the next few days."

"What d'you mean?" I asked.

But he'd gone.

"It can't just be the cat!" I heard Sarah say crossly from outside.

And then she fell through the door. She picked herself up, and gave a blood-curdling scream.

It was only then that I realised what Genie had meant by leftovers. You see, the elephant's head and trunk were suspended over my desk, just floating there near the ceiling.

With no elephant on the end of them.

Chapter 8
Dream Time?

"It was just a dream," I said soothingly to Sarah the next morning in the kitchen. I gave a careless laugh. "I mean, how could I possibly have had an elephant in my bedroom? Or even a bit of elephant."

"It was horrible!" Sarah said with a shudder. "I can't even bring myself to go into your room now."

"That's good ... er ... that's all right," I said. "I should leave it a few days before you even try."

I'd had a right to-do with her the night before. I'd had to get Genie out again, freeze-frame Sarah, then put her into her room and convince her that she'd had a nightmare.

I'd also had to persuade her not to tell Dad about it. I didn't want him to know because he'd have just marched her straight into my room to prove there was nothing there.

Sadly there still was something – a pair of grey, flappy ears, a trunk and half an elephant's head.

"So many strange things have happened lately that I don't understand," Sarah said. "There was that awful little fat man I thought I saw and ..."

She suddenly stopped speaking. I was at the sink, and I turned to see why.

The answer was, she stopped speaking because she'd disappeared!

I screamed. And at that minute her friend Helen knocked on the door to walk to school with us.

I looked under the table for Sarah, just in case, and then I looked in the broom cupboard.

I knew what had happened, though. Well, it didn't take a genius to work *that* out.

I shouted to Helen that we wouldn't be long, then ran upstairs (just two elephant ears and one elephant eye left), and tapped out Genie.

"Where is she?" I asked. "Where's my sister?"

"She's gone away to think things over," Genie said grandly.

"What d'you mean gone away? Gone away where?!"

"She's halfway across the desert, oh Keeper of the Cockroaches. She is all at sea without a camel." He bowed. "It is to punish her for calling Genie an awful little fat man. She must walk across hot sands for fifty days, then she can return."

I shook my head. "She'll have to return before that!" I said. "People will notice. My Dad will go mad!"

"It is fit punishment, oh Mistress of all the Mooses."

"I'm sure it is," I said. "But my Dad will get the police. And Helen's waiting downstairs and we've got to go to school. Sarah will have to come back *now*."

I tried to sound as if I expected to be obeyed, in a princess sort of way. It must have worked, because after a moment Genie sighed heavily. He made some movements with his hands, pointing downstairs.

"She is back," he said sulkily.

I said thanks, tapped him back in, then went down to the kitchen, letting in Helen on the way.

Sarah was sitting at the table watching breakfast telly and looking dazed.

"Oh, a programme about the Sahara desert," I said, switching it off pretty smartish.

"Sahara desert ..." Sarah said in a stunned voice. "Awful place. Burning hot ... you could smell the dry sand ..."

"What's up with you?" asked Helen.

"She's just been watching a very realistic programme about the desert," I said brightly.

I didn't feel bright at all. I felt like dying on the spot.

"Nothing but burning sand ..." Sarah droned on.

I poked her to get up. "Come on, then. School!"

Helen lent towards Sarah, frowning. "It must have been a *very* realistic programme," she said, "because you've got sand in your hair!"

I froze, then slapped Helen on the back. "You like to have a laugh, don't you!"

"No, really, she has. There, look! I can ..."

I grabbed Sarah's school bag and pushed both of them out of the door. We'd got as far as the gate when I suddenly made up my mind. It had been a close thing. *Too* close.

"Just a sec. I've forgotten something," I said, and went back into the house and came out carrying the blue box.

"What have you got that for?" Helen asked. Sarah was still all dozy.

I breathed deeply. I'd decided. It was all very well having a genie, but quite honestly it was just too much to cope with.

"We pass the church hall on the way to school, don't we?" I said. I waved the box. "I'm giving this to their next jumble sale."

Other Barrington Stoke titles available:-

What's Going On, Gus? by Jill Atkins 1-902260-10-4

Bungee Hero by Julie Bertagna 1-902260-23-6

Hostage by Malorie Blackman 1-902260-12-0

Starship Rescue by Theresa Breslin 1-902260-24-4

Ghost for Sale by Terry Deary 1-902260-14-7

Sam the Detective by Terrance Dicks 1-902260-19-8

Billy the Squid by Colin Dowland 1-902260-04-X

Kick Back by Vivian French 1-902260-02-3

The Gingerbread House by Adèle Geras 1-902260-03-1

Virtual Friend by Mary Hoffman 1-902260-00-7

Tod in Biker City by Anthony Masters 1-902260-15-5

Wartman by Michael Morpurgo 1-902260-05-8

Extra Time by Jenny Oldfield 1-902260-13-9

Screw Loose by Alison Prince 1-902260-01-5

Life Line by Rosie Rushton 1-902260-21-X

Problems with a Python by Jeremy Strong 1-902260-22-8

Lift Off by Hazel Townson 1-902260-11-2

If you would like more information about the **BARRINGTON STOKE CLUB**, please write to:- Barrington Stoke Club, 10 Belford Terrace, Edinburgh, EH4 3DQ or visit our website at:- www.barringtonstoke.co.uk